Famous Folk Tales

retold by **Saviour Pirotta** ◆ illustrated by **Alessandra Fusi**

Starry Forest Books

The Legend of John Henry

Pecos Bill

Paul Bunyan

THE LEGEND OF JOHN HENRY

JOHN HENRY was a giant of a man: tall and proud as a mountain, and just as solid. Steady as a rock, too, with rock-hard determination. You ask anybody in West Virginia. They'll tell you that there never was, never will be a better man than John Henry.

John Henry cleared the way for railroad tracks. He was so able, folks say he was born with a hammer in his hands. He could work more than ten men and never need a rest.

John Henry was a steel-driving man. He'd hammer a spike
into solid rock, fill the hole with dynamite, and ... *BOOM!*
Blast that mountain wide open.

One day, a new steam-powered drill chugged up the mountain. It puffed like a dragon, its whistle shrieking, *Get out of my way!*

John Henry knew the machine meant the end of his job, and all his friends' jobs, if it drilled faster than the men.

"Let's race," he challenged the driver. "See who gets through the mountain fastest."

"On your mark, get set, go!" Sparks flew as John Henry swung his hammer, cleaving deeper and deeper into the mountain until there was only a pinpoint of sunlight behind him.

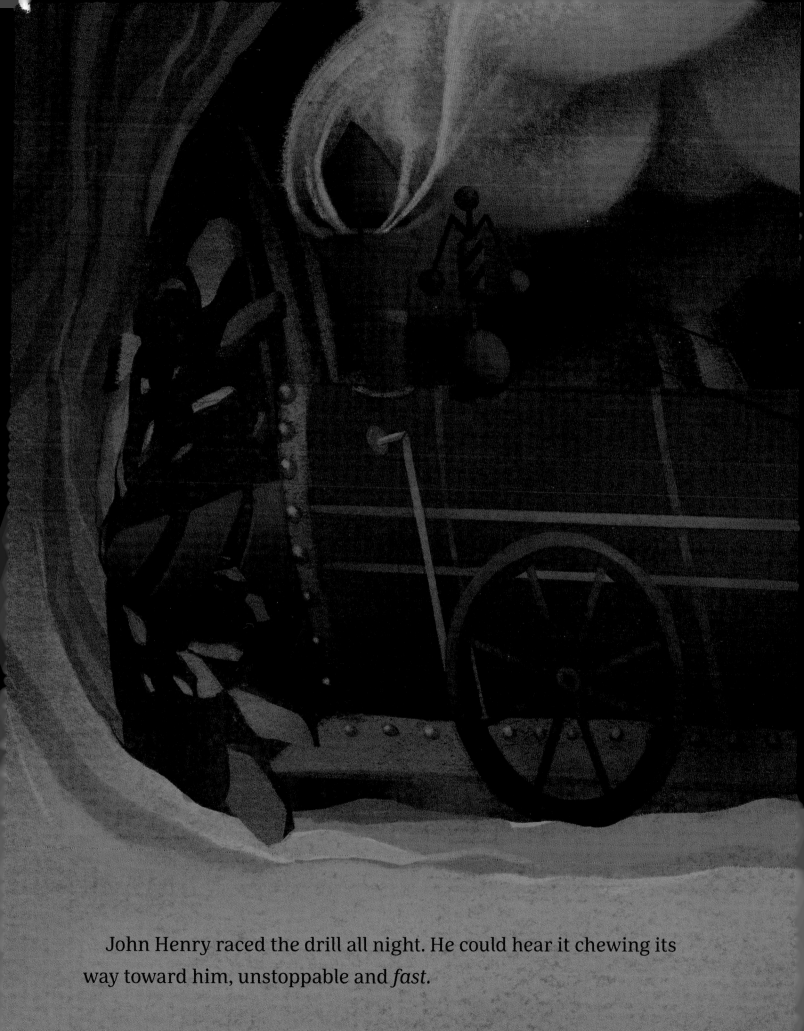

John Henry raced the drill all night. He could hear it chewing its
way toward him, unstoppable and *fast*.

But not as fast as John Henry. At sunrise, he cut through the last bit of rock between him and the engine. He walked right past it, into the fresh morning air. Beat it fair and square.

"Hooray for John Henry!" his friends hollered. John proved mind, muscle, and heart can't be defeated.

Every train that roars by still pounds out the steady beat of
his hammer, praising John Henry, the steel-driving man.

Pecos Bill

TEXAS is so big, even its stories stretch a mile. Take Pecos Bill. Folks say a pack of coyotes raised Bill. He grew up wild. When he howled, the creatures understood him, and he understood them too.

Pecos Bill and his coyote family were right fond of one another.
The night Bill left to be a cowboy, they all howled sadly. The stars fell
like tears, till only one was left. That's why Texas is the Lone Star State.

Bill was cold that night. When he heard rattling, he reckoned it
was his teeth chattering. Then he saw it: the meanest rattlesnake
in Texas, coiled around him. Bill grabbed it and swung it dizzy.
After that, the snake became Bill's lasso. They got along dandy.

A cowboy needs a horse. Bill being Bill, he jumped on the wickedest one he could find. The horse took off at full speed and flew Bill over the Arctic Circle, under Chile, and through the Grand Canyon. But Bill stuck on like a burr.

A horse like that is never really tamed. Folks say he ate only dynamite, and he wouldn't let anybody but Bill ride him. He was so fast, Bill named him *Lightning*.

One evening, Pecos Bill heard a loud "*Yee-haw!*" He saw a woman riding a giant catfish down the rapids, one-handed. Bill's heart went *bumpity-bumpity-bump.* Here was the woman for him! Brave, beautiful, and wild.

"Want some beans?" hollered Bill.

"Sure!" shouted the woman.

"My name's Slue-Foot Sue," she said. "And you're Pecos Bill. I've heard of you and your lightning-fast horse."

Bill was a goner. "Will you marry me, Slue-Foot Sue?" he asked, starry-eyed.

"Sure," replied Sue. "If you let me ride that horse of yours to the wedding."

"W-e-l-l," drawled Bill, shaking his head. "Okay."

On Bill and Sue's wedding day, the sky was a peculiar coppery green. Sue wore a dress with a springy bustle. The moment she sat on Lightning, that cantankerous horse threw her sky high. Then down she came, landing on her bustle with such a *boing* that she bounced right back up again, this time so high that her head knocked against the moon.

Pecos Bill saw an inky black funnel barreling toward him. "A cyclone!" he shouted. He lassoed the cyclone, hopped on top, and scooped up Slue-Foot Sue.

"Yee-haw!" whooped Sue, delighted. She and Bill rode the cyclone
till it wore itself out. They slid to the ground.

"Are you all right, darlin'?" Bill asked.

"Sure!" said Sue. "But I'll never ride that horse of yours again."

PAUL BUNYAN

PAUL BUNYAN was the biggest baby ever born. He weighed
one hundred pounds, and his beard was so thick that his Ma combed it
with a pine tree. His Pa made him a cradle big as a canoe and put it in the harbor.
Paul rocked so hard, he caused a tidal wave that swept two villages out to sea.

Paul grew to be more massive than a house. His stride was a mile wide.

"Son," said his Pa. "A fella big as you should help folks."

So Paul became a lumberjack. He cleared land for people to plant crops and build roads. Paul's axe was so big that he dragged it behind him and created the Great Lakes.

Paul hired the Seven Axe Men to work with him. They were ten feet tall and could pop their buttons in one inhale. Still, the Axe Men had to hustle to chop down trees as quick as Paul.

Hot Biscuit Sally was the cook. Paul built her a griddle big as an ice rink. The Axe Men greased it by skating on it with giant chunks of bacon tied to their boots.

One winter was so cold, words froze. Paul dug a baby ox out of the snow.

"Aww," cooed the Axe Men. "Let's call him *Babe*."

Paul thought Babe was blue with cold. But even after Babe thawed by the fire, he remained a bright blue.

Babe grew up to be titanic. He was longer than forty spades and heavier than sixty barrels of fish. It took a crow all winter to fly from one horn to the other. Every day Hot Biscuit Sally made Babe his favorite sandwich: ten acres' worth of sweet clover stuffed between giant flapjacks.

Some loggers said to Paul, "This river twists and turns so much that our logs get jammed. Can you help us?"

"Sure!" said Paul.

Paul hitched Babe to one bend of the river. The big blue ox dug in his hooves and p-u-l-l-e-d harder than any ox ever did before or ever will again.

Finally, with a *SPLASH!* and a *ROAR!* Babe pulled that river straight as an arrow. "Hooray!" the loggers cheered. "Thank you!"

But Paul couldn't stop to talk. He was chasing Babe, who just
kept walking, probably looking forward to a sweet clover sandwich.